DORMROOM SEX STORIES
EXPLICIT DIRTY EROTICA SHORT STORIES

SAGE YARBER

Xplicit Press
Erotica Fiction

CHAPTER 1

THE AGE OF WISDOM

NINETEEN-YEAR-OLD BAETHAN HAINSWORTH still wasn't sure why she'd agreed to tutor her roommate's cousin. True, twenty-year-old Kazan Dern was hot. White blond hair, jade green eyes. At just under six feet, he was the shortest member of the UEC basketball team, and easily the best looking. And, according to Melody Dern, he was one bad grade away from being academically ineligible to play. Baethan's advanced placement in her mathematics courses made her, in Melody's opinion, the perfect choice to help.

With her soft Southern accent and slender body, Baethan looked like someone that men would trip over themselves to hit on. She, however, prided herself on being antisocial, preferring her books to an actual company. It didn't help that she kept her burnt umber curls short for convenience and didn't play up her beautiful arctic blue eyes or fine features with make-up. Or, at least in her opinion, it did help since she didn't want attention sent her way. On the rare occasions, she felt the need to involve a second party to scratch an itch; she'd call one of her fuck buddies and keep it simple. Granted, all three of her 'friends with benefits' spent more time-fighting trolls and orcs in fantasy-land than they did talking to girls, but she was okay with that. Truth be told, she enjoyed the occasional stroll through cyber-land make-believe. She knew how others saw her and had long since stopped caring.

A knock at her door drew Baethan from her thoughts. She scowled and gave herself a quick once over. She didn't actually care what she looked like, just that she was decent. Pale green shorts and a clingy t-shirt. No holes. No stains. She shrugged. Good enough. She got up and let in her student.

"I'm never going to get this," Kazan threw down his pencil in disgust.

"You'd think getting kicked off the basketball team and losing your scholarship would be appropriate motivation not to give up," Baethan crossed her arms and rolled her eyes. Kazan was exactly like she'd thought. Lazy and unmotivated. They'd only been working for a half-hour and he was already giving up.

"Excuse me?" Kazan's eyebrows shot up.

Apparently, he wasn't used to anyone talking to him so bluntly. Well, Baethan wasn't going to sugarcoat for some jock who thought the world should be handed to him on a silver platter. "Maybe you need to focus on the fact that you get to keep playing with your little ball if you do well." At Kazan's petulant look, she asked, exasperated, "How in the hell did you ever graduate high school?"

He grinned, the expression completely transforming his

face into the one that girls swooned over. "I banged my teachers."

Baethan closed her eyes, trying to control her temper. When she opened them, she realized that Kazan was staring at her, his gaze running over her body with an appreciative light in his jade eyes. An idea formed in her mind.

"I think positive reinforcement may be the solution. So, how about this?" She crossed one long leg over the other, noting how he followed the movement. This could work. "For every answer you get right, I'll remove an article of clothing. Get it wrong, and I'll put something back on."

Kazan's jaw dropped. Apparently, he held the common opinion that girls like her were mousey and shy.

"I'm a nerd, Kazan, not a nun," Baethan couldn't stop herself from smirking.

Twenty minutes later, Kazan had completed six questions. The first had been right and Baethan had pulled off her top. The second and third had been wrong, the last three right. Baethan was down to her panties and bra as she went over his seventh problem. When she reached behind her to unclasp her bra, she felt heat rising to her cheeks, less from what she was doing and more from the darkening of Kazan's eyes. When her panties followed a few minutes after, Baethan was shocked to feel that the cotton was damp.

"Shit," Kazan stared and Baethan felt a flush that had nothing to do with embarrassment. With it came a rush of power.

Baethan spread her legs, letting Kazan get a good look at her pink, glistening folds. She shaved because she preferred it, but was suddenly glad that she did. "Let's raise the stakes." She passed over a paper with five more difficult problems. "Get four out of these five right and I'll masturbate in front of you."

Kazan made a strangled sound and searched her face, she assumed, for the truthfulness of her statement. He must've found it because he grabbed the paper and bent over it to work.

As she graded it ten minutes later, she felt Kazan's eyes on her and heat pooled in her stomach at the thought of what she was about to do. A thrill went through her as she marked his test and leaned back in her chair.

She closed her eyes and let her hands roam over her body, brushing her breasts, skimming over her stomach and down to her thighs. One hand settled between her legs, the other trailing back up to her breast. She knew her body well, could bring herself to orgasm quickly, and so let her hands move from memory.

Palm rubbing over her clit, two times back and forth, two up and down, two circles. Then a slide down to slip her two middle fingers into her pussy. Repeat as her other fingers worked over her nipple. Repeat. Repeat. And again.

She shuddered as she climaxed, pleasure washing over her.

"Fuck, that was hot," Kazan's voice made Baethan open her eyes. Kazan was openly rubbing the growing bulge at his crotch. "What do I get if I get an 'A' in the class?"

Baethan wailed as Kazan pounded into her, his cock hitting that spot inside her that made her see stars. Her legs were splayed wide, bouncing as each thrust drove her body into the bed. Her hands scrabbled at his skin, nails raking down his back leaving red marks in their wake. He hissed, lowering his head to nip at the soft flesh of her breasts.

She cried out again, every muscle in her body trembling with the intensity of the sensations running through her. Her back arched, her hips twitching as she tried to meet his thrusts. Her muscles refused to obey, her arms falling open, her entire body going limp as her nerves overloaded.

"Fuck," Kazan let out a long, drawn-out groan as he buried himself deep inside, body stiffening as he came. He collapsed on Baethan, panting. After a moment, he gathered enough energy to roll off her.

They lay side-by-side as they caught their breath. The late afternoon light shone through the window, glistening off their sweat-slicked skin. Kazan broke the silence, turning his head to look at Baethan as he spoke. "So, I set up my schedule for next semester. How are you at chemistry?"

CHAPTER 2

A FIRST TIME FOR ANYTHING

"I AM TELLING you Sarah you really do need to get laid. You are just too damn stressed and it is starting to show because you are snapping at everyone." Casey looked a Sarah. She could tell that Sarah was about to come apart at the seams and start bawling. Sarah looked at Casey.

"Sarah all I am saying is that you need to take some time for yourself and let go for a night. I am not saying that you have to be with the man forever for God's sake, we are sopho- more's in college. We really both have too much invested into college to mess up now. However this weekend you are going to take some time and go out with us or you are going to go out on a date with one of the guys on campus, it is up to you."

Sarah knew that Casey was right, she really did need to do something that was out of the ordinary. But she did not want Casey to know that she had never had a date, even in high school. She was always trying to please her parents, getting the best grades she could. But she had to admit another girl's night just did not seem like fun at all. She had to admit that a date with a guy for a night sounded like fun, and nothing serious had to happen. It could just be a friendly dinner and dancing.

"Alright, I tell you what. I will go on an actual date with a guy from the college if that means that you will get off of my back about trying to relax," Sarah laughed. Shocked at what Casey had just heard she paused for a moment. "You're on babe. I will ask Eric to go out with me to a dinner and dance, and if you want, we can double date. It is all in your court."

Sarah had to admit she felt like Casey did not think that she could actually go out on a date and she was going to prove her roommate wrong, one way or another. But who would she actually have as a date for the night? Sarah was really going to have to think about this one, but she knew she only had one day until the weekend. She was definitely going to need a miracle for this one.

As she walked to her last lecture, she thought about what Casey had said about needing to let go for a night. She was right, but Sarah was too proud to admit that. She knew that all of her life she had taken her schooling too seriously. She did not even go to her prom, because she wanted to make sure all of her work was perfect and she had been able to do all of the extra credit possible.

. . .

Just as she entered the lecture room, she looked around the enormous room for a seat. She had to admit this was one of her fullest classes she had this year, so finding a seat was always a problem.

Then she found one, and there was no one sitting next to the one that was empty. Sitting in that seat she bent over to get her pens and book out. As she began to sit up her pen rolled away from her. Trying to hurry to catch it, she noticed someone was reaching down to get it for her. As she looked up, she noticed that it was a guy. She had not seen him in this class before, but damn she had to admit he was hot. His short black hair was slicked back and from what she could see he had a decent build and she had to admit she loved the look of his hauntingly green eyes.

"Oh, thank you," she said. Sarah could not help but flutter her eyes just a little bit. There was something about him that gave her the feeling that this would be a great guy to go out with tomorrow. Hell, she might even ask him out tonight.

Looking at the seat that was empty next to her, he smiled. Putting his bag down he sat in the open seat. Sarah could feel the heat rise in her cheeks. As they sat through Psychology she could not help but feel the heat of his stare, and she had to admit she liked it. What was she thinking? She could not help but look over at him times during class. After class just as they were about to get out, he turned to her and said, "Aaron ... my name is Aaron. I was wondering if you would like to go out for coffee after we get out of here?"

"Sure, let's go. I am going to call my roommate and let her know not to expect me for a while. It is just something that we do since we take turns cooking. That way she does not have a plate out for me if I am not going to be there."

Dialing Casey's number Sarah knew that she was still going to be in her class so she just left a message. "Hey Casey, I am going out with one of my classmates for coffee. Don't worry about dinner for me, I will just get something when I get home." With that, she put her iPhone in her back pocket. She was excited she was actually going out with a guy. Sure, it was for coffee, but in her book, she would call it a date. Sarah smiled at the thought - her first actual date with a guy.

Heading to the parking lot, they stopped at her car and put her book bag in the backseat. "Would you mind if we walked? That way I can get my walk-in for the day," Sarah asked. "Sure," Aaron smiled looking in to her eyes; he could not help but get lost in her eyes. "Thank you for agreeing to go out with me for coffee. I know that you do not usually go out, or at least that is what I have been told by classmates. But I figured it was because you had too much invested into your education, which to me means that you take pride in your education which is something that I really like about you."

. . .

He knew that he would be taking a risk just by reaching down for her hand, but he had to admit that he wanted to see what she would do. To his surprise, her small hand stayed in his hand and she did not pull away from him at all.

When they arrived at the campus coffee shop, Sarah loved how when you first opened the door you were greeted with the many different aromas of coffee. Sitting down at a table, they talked for hours. Before they knew it, it was going on at 8 pm. Looking into Sarah's eyes Aaron took a minute. "Hey listen, I have had a great time with you tonight and I was wondering if you would like to come to my house for a little bit and have a drink or two?"

He knew it may be too soon to ask her to come to his place but he could not let her go tonight. There was something about her that was incredible. Sarah could not imagine that this guy was asking to spend more time with her, as no one had done that not even in high school. Since she was the nerd in class, the only time they wanted anything was to try and get her to do their homework for a price.

However, she could see that there was something more that she could not put her finger on. What was it about him that was compelling her to go with him?

"Alright, let's go."

As they walked back to the campus, she felt a little nervous. She had never done anything like this before. What was she doing? She had to admit in some strange way she wished that she could say that she went over to some guy's house for the night, but she knew that they were just going to his place for a few drinks and she would be going home. But at least she could tell Casey that she went out with a guy. She smiled at that thought. She loved how she felt and she really wished that the feeling would never go away.

They continued to walk to his place. He lived on 1st and Culberson, and it was a small place but it was nice. She could tell that he was a decent guy. He was respectable, which was something that wasn't noticeable with all guys. She was having a great night. He had made screwdrivers and she had to admit she loved them. "Thank you for a great night. I hope that we can do this again," she said. One thing that she did not want to tell him was that she really did not want the night to end, but how could she stay if he did not ask her to stay?

She had never been one to even have any interest in men, let alone wanting to stay with them for a night. But there was something about him that made her want to stay, and for a change do something that she normally would not. She was going to get laid tonight at least once. Sitting on his suede couch, she finished her drink. She was amazed at how much that one drink went down too smooth. Setting her glass down on the glass coffee table, she slowly slid across the couch getting closer to Aaron.

·   ·   ·

Aaron did not notice it right away, and then when he did catch her moving he grinned. "Did she want to stay the night with him?" he thought. This was going to be the best night ever for both of them, and he would make sure of that. When he finished his drink he stood up taking her hand and leading her to the bedroom. He began kissing her neck and slowly running his hands up and down her body. Damn, she was amazing.

She stopped him for a minute, "Wait, there is something that I need to tell you before we get in to this too much." Looking down at her, he wondered what she had to tell him. "I'm well ... a virgin." She could feel the heat rise up in her cheeks. She was embarrassed to say it, but she wanted to make sure he knew so that there were no surprises.

"That is okay, I promise you that I will be gentle and it is not going to hurt like most women say that it does." Taking his time to strip all of her clothes off of her he admired every inch of her body.

There was just something that surprised him that she was a virgin. He thought that she would have been with someone. It is not often that you find a virgin in college. But he was going to make sure that this was the best night ever for her. He did not care at all that she had never been with a man; in fact, that made him feel special that she chose him.

Leading her to his bed, he made sure she was comfortable. Taking his time, he spread her legs, putting his body between them, but he did not push his shaft in her womanhood yet. He slowly kissed and caressed her body, taking the time to make sure that she was fully relaxed. He knew that if she was not relaxed there was a chance that she would not only be sore but have some tearing as well. He began to play with her breasts, flicking her nipples with her tongue. He could tell that she was new to the feeling of man. Everything he did, she either jumped or squirmed. But he had to admit that really did get to him and make him want her more. But he also knew with the little bit of foreplay that he was doing to her, her ability to hold out on climaxing was not going to happen. When she came for him, she was not going to be able to hold back at all.

When he knew that she was totally relaxed, he whispered in her ear, "Are you sure you want to go through with this?" He waited for a moment. Then he heard her say in a raspy voice, "Yes." Taking a minute to adjust himself he slowly entered her core, using his other hand to run up and down her leg to take her mind off of any possible uncomfortable feeling that she may have. Then he began pumping his cock into her at a slow but steady rhythm. He could tell that she was getting used to it, as she wrapped her legs around his waist.

"That's it, baby," he loved the feel of her legs wrapped around his waist holding her against him.

He could feel her getting close to climaxing. As she began to arch her body, he heard her moan and it began to get louder. Then he felt it; she had climaxed, but she was still going. He increased the speed until he climaxed. She looked up at him.

. . .

"So that is what all of the hype is huh? Damn that was good," she thought. She definitely would be doing that again with Aaron. "I hope I was not too bad," she said. Aaron laughed. "No not at all," he smiled looking down at her. "In my opinion you were awesome, and I hope this is something that we can do more often."

Sarah laughed," You bet your ass it will."

CHAPTER 3

MY FRESHMAN YEAR OF COLLEGE

I HAD NOT BEEN OUTSIDE of Garrett, Iowa that often. The small town was one of those that exported corn and football players. I fell into the latter category. All my life I had heard how I was going to be the next big thing in football. I had speed and size that was almost unable to be matched. This helped me with the ladies in High School as I seemed to be the most sought-out jock in school. I was given a full scholarship to one of the top schools.

The three National Championships in four years were one of the huge benefits that I saw from joining the football team and to attend school there. I was getting moved into my dorm, and I had to admit that the school alone was almost as big as most of Garrett. I was in for a big shock when I arrived. I was taken aback by the immense amount of traffic that surrounded the school. I met my new room-mate Danny who too was a football jock. Danny seemed to be a rather decent guy but was still just as conceited as most jocks are and thought the world revolved around him

.   .   .

It was our first night in the dorm. The entire dorm was holding a block party as a way for the students to get to know one another. It was a co-ed dorm so we thought it would be a good chance to hook up with some chicks.

We went to the party and were hanging out when a couple of girls came up and started to make idle talk with us. I was attracted to the redhead that was talking up a storm with me. She was telling me her life story and all I was able to think about was how I wanted to head back to one of our places and get to know her in a whole new way. All I managed to get out of the conversation was that her name was Denise and that was pretty much it. Finally, I made the suggestion that we head off somewhere and make use of one of our rooms. I was trying my best to be subtle even though I had very dirty thoughts going through my head. Finally, she spoke up and said that she wanted to take me back to her room and have wild animal-like sex with me. This was all I needed to hear and I headed with her off to her room to see what kind of trouble that we could get into We made her way to her room, but her roommate was trying to study. Denise tried to ask her to leave but she said something about it was her room as well and that she was not going to go anywhere.

Denise told her that was fine and that she could stay but to know that she was going to fuck me wildly and that if she did not like it then now was the time to leave. Again her roommate was not giving in, so Denise began to undress me.

I now had added pressure that I was going to have to perform in front of her roommate. I began to nurse on her tits. I had learned that most women were very sensitive in this area and that the least bit of stimulation would send them into a new dimension of pleasure. I could tell that Denise was no exception to this as her cunt began to glisten with the appearance of her juices that were slipping from her recesses. Denise reached down between her legs and began to take some of the juices onto her finger and lick them from it. I was getting hard from the sight of watching this woman slowly frig herself with a couple of fingers. I reached up with a free hand and began to twist and pull on her other nipple this sensation was getting her wetter to the point that she had a spurt shoot from her cunt and splash onto her leg. I took this as a sign that she was more than ready for me to penetrate her and give her the pounding that she was so desperate for. I laid her onto her back and was mounting up on her when I looked out the corner of my eye and noticed that her roommate was not working anymore and had actually began to play with herself through her panties. I saw a wet spot that had formed on them and took this as a clue that she enjoyed what she was seeing. I took the next logical step and began to thrust with a bit of force into Denise. While I was doing this the room-mate had gotten up and came over. Denise took the hint and began to lick out the cunt of her worked-up roommate.

I continued the process of thrusting in and out as hard as I could in an effort to make sure that the roommate was getting her to fill of watching a woman get her brains fucked out of her. I got ready to hit the point of no return and without a second's notice; I began to cum inside of Denise. I was planning on putting the load on her tits, but this was a great alternative. Anything beat an old gym sock in my room so I was not going to complain. As I was giving Denise a cream pie surprise, her roommate released it as well. This was awesome to see that the bookworm had a little of a kink side to her that she was not eager to admit to in the open. I finished up and cleaned myself up and headed back to the party. I had accomplished my mission and when I returned to the party, I had not seen my roommate; I assumed he had been just as lucky.

When I headed back to my dorm room, I walked in to see a young blonde straddling Danny reverse cowgirl style and getting every inch of Danny shoved into her. The best part was that they did not stop and kept going almost as if I was not even there; I figured I could at least see how the show ended. I was impressed that he had just as impressive amount as I did. And yet he was not afraid to show it. I had a feeling this was going to be an awesome school year and that I and Danny were going to be getting our fill of pussy.

CHAPTER 4

MY ROOMMATE'S BOYFRIEND

"THANK God my roommate's not here," I laughed over the phone. In a few minutes, my boyfriend Anthony would be joining me in my college dorm room. I ended the call with him and rushed off into the shower to take a quick bath.

Within a few minutes, there was a knock at the door. "You know you I had left the door open for you right?"

I pulled him into the room quickly before anyone could see us. What we were doing was wrong and totally unacceptable. Anthony was Karla's boyfriend and she would die knowing that her boyfriend was sleeping with her roommate.

"How long do we have?"

I had been secretly having an affair with my roommate's boyfriend. Today we had decided to do a little quickie between classes. I was sure that we'd be able to get away with it since Karla would be in class the whole morning. Whenever she had back-to-back classes, she NEVER came to the dorm room. And so nothing would change today, I assumed.

"God, you smell good,"

He wrapped his arms around me and pulled me closer Anthony's huge masculine body was something that most college girls lusted after. He was a strikingly handsome young man with a great sense of humor. His lips soon captured mine as he swept me away with a hot passionate kiss that seemed to leave my head spinning. Our tongues danced together in the heat of the moment our hands roamed over each other's bodies.

I yelped a little when he gripped firmly onto my buttocks and squeezed them between the palms of his hands. His kiss intensified, and soon we practically ripped off each other's clothes desperate to feel the nakedness of our bodies in sweet harmony.

He scooped up my naked body in his arms and carried me over to the small twin-sized bed in the room. My heart thudded in anticipation of penetration. I wanted him, needed him, inside and out. Anthony didn't leave me needy for too long, he soon began stroking my inner thighs with the warmness of his wicked tongue. The closer he got to my temple of delight the more I became aroused, one more minute of torture and I'd lose my mind.

He finally parted my legs and exposed my dripping wet pussy. "Oh, God Tony!" I squealed as he lapped at my juices. His tongue moved from the slit of my pussy upwards onto my swollen bud. Another moan escaped my lips as he wrapped his tongue over and around my clitoris, stimulating me further.

He continued to lick every inch of my hungry wet pussy, sucking at it feverishly, taking my tender flesh with his mouth, and licking off all its juices. My body quivered as sensations coursed through my entire being. I cried out in ecstasy, clenching my teeth together and gripping the sheets as he began darting his tongue into my slit. Each time he pulled out his tongue slowly, tiny spasms shot through my pussy.

My body moved involuntarily, completely controlled by my desire to climax. Gripping the back of his head firmly, I locked his face between my legs. He continued licking and sucking, making slurping noises as he went along. His tongue massaged my clitoris as he occasionally tugged and bit it, bringing about an unimaginable sensation.

His fingers soon followed and he penetrated my core with three of his long manly fingers. Over and over, he slammed his fingers into my wetness while his tongue caressed my juicy wet pussy, bringing me closer and closer to my earth-shattering climax.

I began bucking my pussy against his lips, rotating my pelvis, as his tongue massaged my clitoris and his fingers fucked my pussy. Over and over he continued to pleasure me.

Finally, with a loud moan, I summited my earth-shattering climax; coating his tongue with my sweet juices. His tongue swept through my moist heat as he licked all of my juices. When he released my clitoris, I barely had time to breathe before he began to attach once more.

This time his long cock, had found the entrance of my slit and he was stroking my tender flesh with his raw meat.

"Oh, baby...I want it now..." I begged, like a child begging her parent for candy. And so Anthony did give me my candy, a big hard cock thrusting into my wetness, relentlessly without mercy.

I moaned and begged for more, as he rammed hard into my pussy, burying himself to the hilt with each hard thrust.

His huge cock seemed to be slamming into me and making contact with the inner walls of my pussy with each thrust.

As my moaning increased so did the momentum of his thrusts. He was now servicing me with a series of hard, long thrusts. My body spiraled out of control as I struggled to control myself. I was on the brink of another amazing orgasm.

"Let it go, baby," he encouraged as he continued thrusting his cock into my pussy, panting heavily as he went along. We were like two beats running a marathon each one coaching the other to get to their goal which was an amazing orgasm.

Finally, he pulled out and drove his cock deep down into my slit one more time, with a loud thunderous groan. I too closed my eyes, and let out a loud moan, that I was sure could have been heard by the people in the room next door.

"FUCK! JESUS CHRIST!" he groaned as he quickly pulled his cock out of my pussy just in time to splatter his hot load of semen all over my stomach. He groaned as he stroked his full length in the palm of his hands ensuring that all his juices coated my stomach.

I smiled a satisfied grin, as he continued ejaculating the last drop of cum. He collapsed on the bed beside me tired and spent from our brief moment of pleasure. As we lay there, we cuddled each other simmering in the bliss of our ecstasy. Just as we were dozing off into a little sleep, the sound of keys turning in the doorknob startled us.

"Get up QUICK!" I urged him, as he scurried off the bed and tried to launch across the room to the bathroom to hide.

"Tony!" the voice came through the half-cracked door.

"Shit," we were busted. As Karla walked into the room, she gave me a disappointed hurt look. There was not much anger on her face, just hurt. She'd been betrayed by the two people she trusted the most.

"Macy, how could you?"

I sat there, with the sheets wrapped around me, speechless.

CHAPTER 5

FRATERNITY HOUSE SEX PARTY (COLLEGE, CAMPUS, DORM ROOM)

MY NAME IS AMBER THOMPSON, and I am a special doctor. I don't mean special as in I am qualified for one particular type of practice, I mean special in the fact that I am only 18 and have graduated med school. I know that it sounds a little odd, but it is true. I am 18 and a fully accredited doctor. This is a reward that did not come without some massive sacrifice and hard work. I have a high I.Q, but that only gets you so far without the hard work that comes from studying on a regular basis. I had accomplished one of my main goals and I was ready to treat the sick of the world.

It had been a short time since I had got my medical license, maybe a couple of months. I had established myself as being a good doctor to call for minor house calls. My phone rang one night and it was a couple of frat boys that said one of their friends was sick and needed a doctor. I was nearby so I decided to head over. I was not fond of going to frat houses as I had to deal with drunk, horny, obnoxious frat boys who only see a cute little girl and be looking at my ass and tits the entire time. I admit that I had a hot little body, as I had been gifted with natural DD breasts and tried to maintain my figure by working out and watching what I ate. This led to me having very toned legs and a good muscle structure in my body. It was a small price to pay though.

I got to the frat house and from the street could hear the music and smell the beer. I had been to a couple of these parties when I was in college. Actually, it is more proper to say that my roommate dragged me to a couple of these. I walked up to the door and rang the doorbell. I had a feeling that a Neanderthal from back in the Stone Age was going to answer the door. I was shocked to see that it was worse than I thought. At least a Neanderthal had mastered the art of standing. This creature was not even capable of getting that right.

"Someone called and said that a young gentleman was ill, I am the doctor here to look him over."

A little while later, I was lying on the bed tied up with nothing but my bra still on. One of the boys came over and climbed on top of me; he reached up and took one of my breasts out of its prison. He leaned down and began to lick my nipple and suck on it while gently fingering my pussy. It had been a good while since I had a man that had shown such purpose in giving me pleasure slowly. Most of my recent encounters involved me being pounded like a cheap whore and it is over in a matter of minutes. I tried to resist at first but the more I did, the more I realized that I was okay with what was being done and I was not that upset about it. I decided that it was best if I went with it and did what needed to be done in order for me to be able to get them some pleasure and at the same time give me a fucking that I had not had in a long time. I was helpless and had to be at their mercy, this fact alone I think was getting them boned.

As a matter of fact, I was actually getting kind of hot in my snatch at the thought of being a helpless victim at the mercy of these two frat boys. He came up and took the tit that he had freed and began to massage it and then tug on my nipple ring. I had got myself a nipple ring as a gift to myself for when I had finished med school. I figured that it was a decent gift and it showed a little sign of being a rebel, as I was not going to go the way of being the typical doctor. The fact I had decided to start a house call practice allowed me the freedom to not be stuck in a single sitting all day long. Getting back to the action at hand, the frat boy was getting after my nipple and began to finger my hole with a little more aggression. His friend then decided that it was time to get in on the action and came over and got between my legs. I felt the outer tip of his tongue as it began to lick my clit. I was amazed that this young man had hit my G-Spot on the first attempt and hit it with almost a sniper-type approach. His efforts became a little more intense as he dove in with a passion for taking in all of my beauty and essence. I felt his tongue darting in and out of my hole with a rapid pace. I wanted to reach my climax right then and there. The first boy that had been on me took his rigid member and placed it in between my tits; he finished removing my bra and decided that he was going to get a through tit fucking from me. I was not accustomed to this, as I had never had a man do this to me. It was mostly a matter that they simply were not interested as they had more of an interest in my pussy instead. The sensation of his cock between my tits and him squeezing them so as to have my tits encase his enlarged meat was amazing. I never felt anything as pleasurable as that in my whole life. I started to get into the motions that were taking place and knew that before long I was going to get a double reward as I was going to be driven to the edge of ecstasy as well as both of these studs were going to reward me with a thick and creamy load of their man gravy.

The frat boy that had been eating my pussy out quickly changed things up and began to fuck gently my pussy with his erect member. He was not that long, but I could tell that he was thick as hell and that he was used to using this thick tool on a number of women. I could imagine half the women on campus being filled with this large thick piece of meat. Both men were working in unison on me, it was clear that they had one goal in mind and that was to spray their seed inside of me as well as on me before this encounter was even close to being finished. I began to moan uncontrollably as the sensation of these two men taking their turns with me was getting me worked up to the point that I was going to explode and orgasm at a moment's notice.

Without warning, the one that was fucking my tits pulled back and sprayed my face and tits with his thick load. I had cum dripping off of me when I felt a warm sensation up inside of my snatch; I looked up to see the other frat boy finishing up dumping his seed into me. I was a little afraid of being knocked up but was certain that my cycle was still a few days away. I was finally pushed to the point that I had to release. I had held out for as long as I could. It was now time for me to give the both of them something to remember me by. I had always had the ability when it came to my orgasm, to have a rather large and intense release. I unleashed and showed why in college I had gained the nickname of the water hose. There was a large amount of fluid that erupted from me and both men were quite shocked when they saw the intense amount of spray that I produced. There was a knock at the door and one of the other members of the fraternity stuck his head into the room. He informed the men that the hooker that they had ordered was there. The boys had a very strange look on their faces.

CHAPTER 6

THE FRESHMAN

IT WASN'T GOING to be the first time that she had slept with a student. But it was the first time that a freshman taught her a few things about being fucked.

As Eduardo tries the door a third time, he realizes that it is locked. He looks to where Lin, the stunning college professor, late thirties, sits on her desk next to the pile of books he'd helped her carry from her lecture hall. The Latino freshman, a scholarship student of nineteen, from the projects, wonders when she had managed to lock the door; probably while he put the books down. He knows the look on her face. It says that there is something wrapped snuggly between her legs that requires his attention. It also says that she is used to having things her way and that he wouldn't be leaving before fucking her. If it's a fuck she wants then that is exactly what she'll get. But not her way; Eduardo isn't that kind of guy. He's going to fuck her *a la Eduardo* style.

He stands in front of her and pulls her to him, wrapping her legs around his waist. Eduardo rolls her skirt up so that it is just above her hips. Through his jeans, he thrusts towards her cunt gently, teasing her with what he knows she wants. She lifts his shirt, revealing a perfect abdomen. He pushes his shirt back down in mock shyness and steps back a little. His hands are on her panties, pulling them off and letting them drop to the floor. There's a little over twenty minutes before his next class and he intends to be done by then. He didn't come to college to bunk class, no matter the reason.

Lin's cunt is well manicured. This is expected given how well-groomed she herself is. Eduardo can only look at it at first, the perfection of the trim, the suggestion of a hole, the hint of arousal on the tiny clit. He taps it with the tip of his index finger and the cunt immediately comes to life. The entrance to her pussy reveals itself and Eduardo knows that this won't be too much of a struggle, provided that the pampered pussy is prepared for fourteen inches of thick, uncut Latino dick. This is going to be a quickie in every sense of the word. Eduardo hopes to himself that the vagina perched on the mahogany desk will be able to take him into itself quickly.

Lin goes for his belt, trying to free his cock. She bends over towards the dick and bites over the denim. She wants the dick in her mouth. Eduardo hasn't gone hard yet and so nothing gives the size of his dick away. He doesn't want her to know this, the apprehension this would cause would lead to a tightening of her pussy that would require more work than would be possible in the twenty minutes they have. He takes her off his cock and lays her on her back, pulling her legs towards himself. Eduardo pulls her legs apart and then spreads his legs so that he keeps hers open. He undoes his belt and lets his pants drop. Then he pulls down his boxers and wraps a condom over it. He taps his cock on

Lin's pussy and then presses it into her not-yet-wet-enough cunt.

Eduardo slides her towards him a little more so that his cock is almost half inside her. His hands on her knees, a firm grip, he pulls her to him while thrusting forward into her. Her gasps become louder as she starts to realize just how big the dick is that is being sent into her. She wants to see it. Lin tries to lift herself up for a view but Eduardo just sends a few more inches into her so that she can't lift herself off the wood for all the *wood* inside her. He pulls her so completely onto his dick that she has to brace herself on the side of the desk, her knuckles white. Instead of trying to push up, she pushes down into the desk so that her pussy lifts up slightly, giving Eduardo even more access.

Without wasting time, he starts to fuck her elevated pussy deep and hard. His thrusts are deep, downward strokes that end in a lift. She can barely manage to subdue the moans coming from her mouth as she is repeatedly rammed by the thick-dicked freshmen she thought *she* would be seducing. Instead, he is totally working the shit out of her cunt, with no real need for the rest of her. This was unexpected. The size of his dick too was unexpected; the boy possessed a massive cock a thin unthreatening figure. But her cunt has a new respect for the handsome nineteen-year-old she had underestimated.

Her legs lifted up higher now under Eduardo's direction. He pulls her further off of the desk too so that her ass hangs mid-air over the edge. Digging his cock deep into her again, he then pulls her legs together, creating a snug fit around his cock. He hugs her legs tightly and uses his waist and the power in his firm ass to thrust into her. He fucks her through her requests for a break, reading the signs of her dripping cunt ticking so loudly over his dick that it feels like his cock is stuck in a grand clock. The pulsating rhythm has him so close to shooting now that he pushes her legs away from him and down onto her chest and stops moving. He takes a minute to catch his breath.

Soon enough he is fucking her hard again. Without moving her off of his cock, he turns her onto her stomach. His strength is unbelievable. Both hands on either leg at the thigh he has her in what can only be described as a wheelbarrow position, Lin still bracing herself on the sides of the desk. His cock moves in to fill her cunt entirely, a large part of the cock still outside of her though. Lin's pussy ripples in response to Eduardo's efforts to get the rest of his dick inside her. The thick log lodges into it and pulls it towards the outside. Both of them enjoy the counterforce between his dick and her pussy. The friction is *fucktastic,* to say the least.

Eduardo is getting closer to blowing now, closer to his deadline, ten minutes before his next class. He lets Lin's legs drop so that her feet are on the ground. Because of his cock inside her, he has to bend his own knees to make this possible. She shuffles her torso off the desk as well so that her hands are now palm-down on the wood. With her feet on the floor, her hands on the desk, she pushes down onto the cock inside her. Eduardo thrusts upwards, hard. He needs to cum now, and quickly. He takes her hips in hand and pushes into her, circling his cock against the furthest reaches of her pussy. She starts her climax abruptly.

Lifting her one leg, he lets his eyes fall on the area where his cock is pulling down the inner walls of her vagina. This sight is what he needs to fuel his cock on. His fucking becomes rapid ramming. Deep and hard he sends his meat into her, no concern for any part of her that isn't her pussy. She can concentrate on nothing but his cock, the thickness absolutely pulling her cunt apart. She knows to be quiet now but her orgasm is making silence difficult. She bites onto her lip, as Eduardo and his cock don't let up on the work they are doing. It takes him seconds to have her en route to a second orgasm.

He lets the leg drop again, bending her back onto the table completely so that her breasts are on the wood. He raises her ass so that she is on her tiptoes and then sends his cock down and then up deep into her super-wet pussy. His strokes are now harder and deeper than they've been yet. She knows as she gets close to blowing again that Eduardo himself is close to his own climax. His hands are palm-down on her back just above her ass and she arches her back upwards. She looks every bit like a wild cat and Eduardo can't resist giving her another orgasm. Again, he circles her depths with his thickness and again she blows a massive load. He smiles at him as she slumps down now, exhausted.

Eduardo now lifts her legs so that her knees bend mid-air. He locks her legs in this position by pushing against her calves and then locking his own hands onto the edge of the desk. She can move in no direction now, impaled by him. He has nowhere to throw his cock except straight ahead and he does this. He fucks her steadily now with the express goal of bringing himself to a swift ejaculation. Her cunt helps him along by folding and beating, then wrapping its muscular self over his thrusting penis. His cock fights against the vagina's mock attempts to eject it and this resistance unfold to reveal the beginnings of a climax. He's close now.

In a final display of strength, he has her completely off the table now, his hands on her breasts to keep her from dropping to the ground. He lowers himself and her slowly until her hands drop to the floor and he has her legs in a grip again. She walks a little ways in front of herself, looking like an actual wheelbarrow now, much more than she had earlier. Eduardo lets her move around like this while sending his cock into her from where he stands. The strength in her arms is lost quickly though and he lets her climb onto the sofa, a three-seated brown leather couch near the window. He climbs onto her immediately, locks his arms under hers, and proceeds with his vaginal violation.

He breathes into the back of her neck as he digs his cock deep into her and as a result sending her deep into the couch. She feels as though his cock is going to burst through her naval for the strength of his thrusting. Eduardo lifts so high off of her before sending himself back into her that it seems impossible that his cock isn't released from her pussy. But the length of his dick means that he can lift off of her up to ten inches and still have some serious cock inside her.

Deep into her his cock goes as his balls start to flex and wane, ready to shoot his jizz into his shaft. He starts a steady series of grunts and Lin knows that her cunt will receive a reprieve shortly. She lifts her ass slightly so that he can have as much cunt as she has left to offer so that he can cum, quickly.

Lin's pussy wraps tight around Eduardo now, as he seems to be pulling a third orgasm from her. She uses all her strength to create this squeeze, wanting to end this now. She's exhausted.

Eduardo knows that he has given her more than she bargained for and so now he too lets her go, and himself. Her third orgasm is a silent panting, while his grunts are loud and animalistic. His hands are on her hips again as he gives a final deep stab and then stays there until his body stops jerking and his cock starts to go limp. The condom is wrapped in tissue and held in Eduardo's hands as he walks out of her office and down the hall to the bathroom closest to his next lecture. Lin resolves that *this* particular freshman is worth another round and decides that her *books* might need to be carried by him again, *soon*!

ABOUT THE AUTHOR

Sage Yarber is an emerging erotica author of many erotica kinks and sub-genres. Be sure to check out other books and leave a review if this story got you hot!

Visit my blog at Sage Yarber Blog

Join my newsletter for exclusive Sage Yarber Newsletter

Sign up for Free Stories from Xplicit Press Authors

Xplicit Press Author Updates

Like Xplicit Press on Facebook

Follow Xplicit Press on Twitter

Readers: I want to expand a few of the stories to see where the characters can be explored further. If there are any of the stories that you would like to read more about again, I'd love to hear from you!

Keep In Touch
Sage Yarber
info@sageyarber.com

www.ingramcontent.com/pod-product-compliance
Lightning Source LLC
Chambersburg PA
CBHW020422150626
46554CB00014B/2414